T.E.A.M. Rudolph and the Reindeer Games

Silver Dolphin Books

An imprint of Printers Row Publishing Group
10350 Barnes Canyon Road, Suite 100, San Diego, CA 92121
www.silverdolphinbooks.com

Printers Row Publishing Group is a division of Readerlink Distribution Services, LLC.
Silver Dolphin Books is a registered trademark of Readerlink Distribution Services, LLC.

All notations of errors or omissions should be addressed to Silver Dolphin Books, Editorial Department,
at the above address. All other correspondence (author inquiries, permissions) concerning the content of this
book should be addressed to: info@characterarts.com

Produced by:
Jokar Productions, LLC, Redondo Beach, CA
www.jokarproductions.com
Adapted by Joe Troiano

ISBN: 978-1-68412-078-9

Manufactured, printed, and assembled in China.
21 20 19 18 17 1 2 3 4 5

T.E.A.M. Rudolph and the Reindeer Games

Adapted by Joe Troiano

Silver Dolphin

The Reindeer Games

Santa looked at the map
on the wall of his shop—
South Pole at the bottom,
North Pole at the top.

"I need to fly faster and further
each Christmas Eve day.
I need to find eight great reindeer
to pull my sleigh."

Then an idea came—the *Reindeer Games*.

A day of activities,

a challenge,

a test,

a friendly competition

to find the best of the best.

Santa turned to the reindeer and said with a grin,

"It's time for the Reindeer Games to begin!

So good luck, try hard, only your best will do,

and I'll pick my team when the games are through."

Dasher

Dancer

One dashed like a flash across the sky.

One danced on top of each cloud passing by.

One pranced proudly as she flew higher than high.

One mixed in tricks no other reindeer dared try.

Prancer

Vixen

Cupid

Blitzen

One reindeer could rocket and then stop on a dime.

One loved flying and flew in a very straight line.

One's hooves roared like thunder whenever he'd climb.

One flew fast as lightning time after time.

Comet

Donner

The Reindeer Games were over and done.
Santa called out, "Gather 'round everyone!"

And then . . .
Santa waved his hand,
called out "Ho Ho Ho,"
and the names of eight reindeer
appeared in the snow.

First Dasher, then Dancer,
then Prancer and Vixen,
then Comet and Cupid,
then Donner and Blitzen.

Two does and six bucks,
the best of the best.
The reindeer who passed
every Reindeer Games test.

Those eight great reindeer
met every day
and helped each other get ready
to pull Santa's sleigh.

Christmas Eve morning,

Santa came to say,

"Today is the day

you will all pull my sleigh.

"Donner and Blitzen will be the first two in line.

So follow their lead and you will all do just fine.

"Now it's time to get ready.

We've got a lot to do.

The children are counting on me,

and I'm counting on you."

So they pulled Santa's sleigh that Christmas Eve night
and were back at the North Pole by first morning's light.

And around the world, boys and girls

woke up and were happy to see,

it was Christmas morning

just as they dreamed it would be.

Rudolph the Red-Nosed Reindeer

Almost a year had passed since that starry night,
since that Christmas Eve when all went right.
And something unusual had happened . . . how?
Well nobody knows,
but a reindeer was born with a ruby-red nose.

His name was Rudolph.
And his nose was a sight—
it wasn't just red, it glowed like a light!

So every time Santa came around
Rudolph covered his nose to make it look brown.

One day, during the Reindeer Games,

Rudolph met a pretty little doe—Clarice was her name.

And when she told him he was the cutest one there,

Rudolph got so excited he flew high in the air.

But when Rudolph and his friends began clowning around
Rudolph's false brown nose fell down to the ground.

Then Fireball called out for all to hear,
"He's . . . Rudolph the Red-Nosed Reindeer!"

The other reindeer teased Rudolph,
they laughed and made fun.
Rudolph got so embarrassed he started to run.

And he didn't stop until . . .

he met an elf named Hermey,

who didn't want to make toys, like the other elves did,

he wanted to be a dentist since he was a kid.

He was a misfit and so was Rudolph—

they were two of a kind.

So these new friends set off

to see what they could find.

What they found was a creature.
A giant! A fiend!
An Abominable Snow Monster
who was meaner than mean.

Then Yukon Cornelius came 'round the bend,

these two lonely misfits had found a new friend.

Yukon knew the Monster was a Bumble,

and Bumbles are mean.

And this Bumble was the biggest

he'd ever seen.

With a mighty swing of his miner's axe,

Yukon whacked the ice, which started some cracks.

And just as the Bumble got to the bay,

the ice broke free and they floated safely away.

They floated to The Island of Misfit Toys,
toys that needed homes with good girls and boys.

Rudolph promised that when he saw Santa again,
he'd ask him to please find homes for them.
You see . . . Rudolph knew he couldn't stay.
He knew his red nose would give them away.

Back in Christmastown the news was grim.

Rudolph's parents and Clarice were out searching for him.

Rudolph knew they were in trouble and had to be saved.

He searched and found them in the big Bumble's cave.

Then Hermey and Yukon arrived in a sled.

They tricked the Bumble

and dropped lots of snow on his head.

Then Yukon tamed that Bumble.

Now he's sweet as can be.

So Santa let the Bumble

put the star on the tree.

But they still had a problem that Christmas Eve.
The fog was too thick for Santa to leave.

Then as Rudolph's nose glowed redder than red,
Santa smiled, then chuckled, and finally said,
"Rudolph with your nose so bright,
won't you guide my sleigh tonight?"

Then the elves packed the presents
into the sleigh.
It was time for Rudolph
to save Christmas Day!

They raced through the fog till the night was done—
until every toy had a home, even the Misfit ones!

And now whatever the weather, Santa knows,
Christmas will never be canceled.
Thanks to brave little Rudolph,
and his beautiful, wonderful ruby-red nose.

T.E.A.M. Rudolph

A year had passed since that foggy night
when Rudolph's red nose had shined so bright.

Santa was reading the list of good girls' and boys' names,
when Comet came to discuss—the Reindeer Games.
"This year will be different—different I say—
every buck, big or small, can join in and play."

"And the does," Mrs. Claus said,
"they can do what bucks do."
"And the elves," said Boss Elf,
"and the Misfit Toys, too."

"Okay," Santa chuckled, "consider it done.
The Reindeer Games are for everyone—
We'll all join *T.E.A.M. Rudolph!*"
Santa said, filled with pride.
"We'll all work together.
We'll all play on one side."

"We'll *Treat Everyone As Members.*
Treat everyone as friends.
Treat everyone with kindness
that just never ends.

"Because just like the snowflakes
that fall Christmas Day,
we're all different and amazing
in our own special way."

REINDEER GAMES

So Dasher and Dancer and Prancer and Vixen,
Comet and Cupid and Donner and Blitzen
all joined T.E.A.M. Rudolph that snowy December.

You can join, too, if you always remember
to shine your light as bright as it goes.
Shine bright, shine bright,
so everyone knows
you're as special as Rudolph
and his ruby-red nose.